WEED KILLERS

BY
JONNY
ZUCKER

ILLUSTRATED BY
KEVIN
HOPGOOD

Titles in the Full Flight Adventure series:

Planet Talent	David Orme
Invaders	Danny Pearson
Alien Exchange	Melanie Joyce
Camp Terror	Craig Allen
White Water	Jane A C West
Infinity Mirror	Roger Hurn
Robot Rampage	Jillian Powell
Stone End Stadium	Richard Taylor
Weed Killers	Jonny Zucker
Dynamite Deputy	Barbara Catchpole

Badger Publishing Limited
Suite G08, Stevenage,
Hertfordshire SG1 2DX
Telephone: 01438 791037   Fax: 01438 791036
www.badgerlearning.co.uk

Weed Killers ISBN 978-1-84926-551-5

Publisher: Susan Ross
Senior Editor: Danny Pearson
Series Editor: Jonny Zucker
Designer: Fiona Grant
Illustrator: Kevin Hopgood

CONTENTS

New words:

gardening

terrifying

sprinted

shrivelled

bargains galore

chaos

Main characters:

Zoe

Nick

CHAPTER 1

Flash

Saturday night.

Five past ten.

Zoe and Nick were at Zoe's house
listening to music.

"Hey, what's that?" asked Nick running
over to the window.

A flash of light had just shot out from
the ground.

Zoe ran to join him and saw it too.
"That was in the park," she said.

"Yeah," nodded Nick, "it must be kids playing with fireworks."

The light flash vanished.

"I bet you're right," replied Zoe.

* * * * *

A week later, Zoe and Nick spotted a brand new garden centre on the high street.

"That went up quickly," said Nick.

"Let's go and take a look," replied Zoe.

"Do we have to?" moaned Nick, "it'll be boring!"

"Come on," said Zoe, grabbing his arm, "it will only take a minute."

The garden centre was massive.

Zoe and Nick walked past the rows and rows of gardening stuff. There were tools and gloves and bird-feeders.

"Everything seems really cheap," said Zoe.

They turned a corner and bumped into a tall woman with sleek blond hair and glassy eyes. She wore a badge saying STAFF.

"Can I help you?" asked the woman.

"When did this store open?" said Zoe, "it seems to have sprung out of nowhere."

"Can I help you?" repeated the woman, her glassy eyes moving from Zoe to Nick and back again.

"Er... we were just..." tried Nick.

"Can I help you?" said the woman for a third time.

"No, we're fine," said Zoe.

She and Nick hurried to the exit.

"That woman was creepy," said Zoe when they were outside.

"Nah," laughed Nick, "she was just boring. That's why she's working in a place like that."

But Zoe felt uneasy.

The store and the woman had spooked her out.

CHAPTER 2

Gardening Gear

Over the next week, garden centre adverts went up all over town. They showed amazingly low prices and bargains galore.

Zoe and Nick were at the bus stop opposite the centre.

"Hey, look!" said Zoe.

"What?" asked Nick.

"The people who are coming out of the garden centre," said Zoe, "they look all glassy-eyed like that woman we met."

"I told you – they're probably just bored," grinned Nick. "They need to go to some decent shops instead!"

Zoe's Mum was just putting on her coat when Zoe and Nick got back.

"Where are you going?" asked Zoe.

"I am just going to nip down to that new garden centre," replied her Mum. "Mrs Jones next door said it's really good value."

"Er, Mum," said Zoe, "you HATE gardening!"

"I know," replied her Mum, "but Mrs Jones said I HAVE to go!"

Zoe and Nick looked at each other.

An hour later, Zoe's Mum came back; her car boot was full of gardening gear. She walked through the kitchen carrying a spade and a shovel.

"Mum, what are you up to?" asked Zoe, looking amazed.

"It is dry," replied her Mum, looking up at the sky, "and the time is near!"

"The time is near for what?" asked Nick.

But Zoe's Mum ignored them and went into the back garden.

Zoe and Nick followed her out.

Zoe's Mum started digging a large hole in the middle of the garden.

"Mum!" cried Zoe, "what are you doing?"

"That is enough!" snapped Zoe's Mum sharply.

She turned to face Zoe and Nick.

Her eyes were glassy and cold. "Get back in the house now!" she snapped.

Special Sale

Zoe's Mum carried on digging the next day and only stopped when the hole was huge.

"This is crazy!" hissed Zoe, "I don't know what's come over her."

Zoe tried to talk to her Mum but her Mum would not listen.

Two days later, her Dad came back from the garden centre and started digging up the front drive.

"Dad!" shouted Zoe running outside, with Nick. "You're rubbish at D.I.Y! What are you doing?"

"It is dry weather and perfect for my needs," replied her Dad. "So leave me alone!"

To Zoe and Nick's horror, his eyes were glassy now too.

"Something very bad is happening round here," said Zoe.

"We need to go back to the garden centre," said Nick. This time he wasn't laughing.

It was getting dark when they arrived at the centre.

It was crowded. At the very back was a long corridor.

Zoe and Nick crept up to it and saw a long line of people.

They were being directed by members of staff towards a large white door on the left. On the door were the words special sale.

The people went through the door looking normal. But when they came out their eyes were glassy and distant.

"What is going on in there?" whispered Nick.

But before Zoe could answer a hand grabbed both of their backs.

It was the female staff member they had seen on their first visit.

"I am glad you two are here!" she said, "It is YOUR turn NOW!"

CHAPTER 4

Digging

"RUN!" shouted Zoe.

She and Nick twisted out of the woman's grasp and sprinted away.

"What are we going to do now?" asked Nick, his face pale with fear, as they burst onto the street.

"We need a plan," replied Zoe.

The next morning, Zoe's parents were making a new and even bigger hole in the back garden.

"Stop it!" pleaded Zoe.

But they ignored her and carried on digging.

"Tonight is the night!" said Zoe's Mum to her Dad.

"Let's get out of here!" hissed Nick.

They ran down the street. Wherever they went, people were digging holes, replacing tarmac with mud and knocking down walls.

Over and over they heard people saying the same thing: "Tonight is the night!".

"We are running out of time," said Nick.

"I know," nodded Zoe. "We have to find out what is going on, and fast!"

They ran to the garden centre but instead of going inside, they crept round the back.

They stopped when they were outside the room with the special sale sign.

They grabbed some bricks and stood on them.

They found themselves looking through a slightly open window into the room. They gasped in shock.

At the far side of the room, a terrifying frothing tree was hitting the people who came inside with its long branches.

As soon as they were hit, the people went glassy-eyed and left the room. Nick lent against the glass.

The window opened fully and Zoe and Nick fell through.

"WHAT IS THE MEANING OF THIS?" screamed the tree.

"YOU TELL US!" shouted Zoe.

"Tonight will see the invasion of the Power Trees from below the Earth!" yelled the tree. "We are taking over the minds of as many people as possible to dig holes and prepare the ground for us! Soon the Earth will be ours!"

"There's no way you'll take over the Earth!" shouted Nick.

"YES THERE IS!" snarled the tree, "and you will help us!"

It laughed in an evil high-pitched tone and shot a branch out at them.

CHAPTER 5

Not Today!

"MOVE!" screamed Zoe.

She and Nick dived out of the way.

The branch missed them by a centimetre.

"YOU WILL OBEY ME!" screeched the tree, lashing out again.

As Zoe and Nick sprang out of the way again, an idea suddenly leapt into Zoe's head.

In a second she reached into her backpack and pulled out a bottle of water.

She uncapped it and threw the water at the centre of the tree.

"NOOOO!" it screamed, its branches waving, twisting and snapping off.

There was a loud bang and the tree suddenly shrivelled to nothing.

"H...h...how did you know to do that?" gasped Nick.

"I remembered my Mum and Dad talking about dry weather being good. I figured the tree must hate rain, so I chucked water at it!"

Inside the garden centre and all over the town there was chaos. The glassy-eyed people had returned to their senses.

They had no idea what had been happening to them.

Back at Zoe's house her parents were standing in the back garden looking shocked.

"What is this hole doing in the garden?" asked her Dad.

"And why is the front drive covered in dirt?" asked her Mum.

"I think that new garden centre had too many special sale offers," replied Zoe.

A week later, Zoe and Nick were walking past the garden centre when a giant tree jumped out at them.

Zoe screamed and reached for her bottle of water, but Nick stopped her.

It was a member of staff from the centre, dressed up as a tree.

"Would you like to become members of the garden centre at a special price?" he asked, hopefully.

"Not today!" replied Nick.

"No," added Zoe, "you're barking up the wrong tree!"

Interesting Plant Facts

The dangerous trees in this story are made up, but some trees and plants can be very dangerous in real life, especially to animals who might eat them.

- *All parts of Yew trees are very poisonous. The Yew is probably the most poisonous tree in Great Britain. The poison does not disappear if leaves fall-off the tree. The poison stays on the leaves even if they fall-off the trees. The poison on Yew trees is very, very strong and an animal can die just a few hours after eating it.*

- *One of the most dangerous plants is Bracken. This is a common plant found on hills. While it is green it is very poisonous. Its roots are the most poisonous part. Some animals eat Bracken, particularly horses. If they eat it for two months they can lose weight, their coats become damaged and they can die.*

- *Luckily, in many areas where horses and other animals live, farmers fence off things like Yew trees and Bracken to stop the animals eating them.*

- *In some areas there are signs warning people to keep their pets away from these trees and plants.*

Questions about the Story

● *How did Zoe and Nick first know that trouble might be ahead?*

● *Why didn't Nick want to go to the garden centre at first?*

● *What did the garden centre adverts promise?*

● *What did Mum return from the garden centre with?*

● *What did the female member of staff do to Zoe and Nick on their second visit to the garden centre?*

● *What exactly were the Power Trees planning?*